For a moment Titus just stood there—frozen in horror.

He had lost the monkey.

Somebody else's monkey.

A monkey that he—Titus—was supposed to be taking care of.

It was a terrible time to be without cousins.

Titus put the little, wooden whistle to his lips and gave three long, desperate blasts.

THE MYSTERY OF THE
CLUMSY JUGGLER

Elspeth Campbell Murphy
Illustrated by Chris Wold Dyrud

Chariot Books™
David C. Cook Publishing Co.

A Wise Owl Book
Published by Chariot Books™,
an imprint of David C. Cook Publishing Co.
David C. Cook Publishing Co., Elgin, Illinois 60120
David C. Cook Publishing Co., Weston, Ontario

THE MYSTERY OF THE CLUMSY JUGGLER
© 1991 by Elspeth Campbell Murphy for text and Chris Wold Dyrud
for illustrations

Cover design by Stephen D. Smith
First Printing, 1991
Printed in the United States of America
95 94 93 92 91 5 4 3 2

Library of Congress Cataloging-in-Publication Data
Murphy, Elspeth Campbell.
 The mystery of the clumsy juggler / Elspeth Campbell Murphy;
illustrated by Chris Wold Dyrud.
   p. cm.—(The Beatitudes mysteries)
 "A Wise owl book"—T.p. verso.
 Summary: Three cousins helping Professor McKay at a medieval fair
are able to collect enough information to trap the thief of a valuable old
Gospel, thus illustrating the Beatitude "Blessed are those who hunger
and thirst for righteousness for they will be filled."
 ISBN 1-55513-897-7
 [1. Beatitudes—Fiction. 2. Cousins—Fiction. 3. Mystery and
detective stories.] I. Dyrud, Chris Wold, ill. II. Title. III. Series:
Murphy, Elspeth Campbell. Beatitudes mysteries.
PZ7.M95316Mxf 1991
[Fic]—dc20

                                                          89-39821
                                                              CIP
                                                              AC

CONTENTS

"Blessed are those who hunger and
thirst for righteousness,
for they will be filled."
Matthew 5:6 (NIV)

1
AT THE FAIR

"Watch this," Titus McKay whispered to his visiting cousins, Sarah-Jane Cooper and Timothy Dawson.

He went up to his father and spoke in a calm voice. "Dad, there's a giant, purple tarantula crawling up your leg."

Without looking up from his clipboard, Professor McKay patted Titus on the shoulder and said, "Good, good. We're doing just fine. Everything is under control."

When the cousins burst out laughing, Professor McKay looked up in surprise. "Oh, hi, kids. Hey, your costumes look great, don't they? Uh—I'm sorry—did you just tell me something?"

"Dad!" cried Titus. "I just told you that

there was this giant, purple tarantula crawling up your leg. And you said, 'Good, good.' "

Professor McKay laughed. "I guess I have been a little preoccupied lately. Remind me never to be in charge of a fair again."

"Uncle Richard, never be in charge of a fair again."

"Thank you, Timothy."

The fair was being held at the university where Titus's father taught. The teachers and students were putting it on, and people were coming from miles around to see it.

In Titus's opinion, any kind of fair was exciting. But this one was especially excellent. That was because it was set up to look something like the fairs people went to five hundred years ago.

The main university square had been divided into little mini-streets. The streets were lined with colorful tents and booths where you could buy all sorts of interesting things. For entertainment, there were singers and dancers and musicians and actors and puppeteers and even acrobats.

The students were dressed up as knights and ladies and townspeople and peasants.

The cousins were dressed up, too. The boys weren't too excited about wearing leotards and tunics. But they figured if the college kids were wearing costumes, they could, too. Besides, the cousins' costumes were Professor McKay's idea, and more than anything else, Titus wanted to help his dad.

Sarah-Jane, of course, was *wildly* excited about wearing a beautiful, long dress. She even had brightly colored ribbons wound in her hair.

She was supposed to be a rich nobleman's daughter, so she kept demanding to be called *Lady* Sarah-Jane. But the boys figured they had to draw the line somewhere.

The cousins were dying to look around. But Titus remembered what they had come to ask his father about in the first place.

"Dad, did you say you had a job for us to do?"

"Yes—well, mostly, I want you to add to the atmosphere of the fair. Walk around and look like five-hundred-year-old children. I mean, like children who lived five hundred years ago."

"Is that it?" asked Titus, trying to keep the disappointment out of his voice. Just walking around didn't sound like much of a way to help.

His father paused. "Well, there *is* one more thing...."

"Detective work?" asked Timothy hopefully. The cousins had a detective club, and solving mysteries was one of their favorite things to do. They didn't really think there would be any detective work to do at the fair, but it didn't hurt to ask.

Professor McKay looked at them in surprise. "As a matter of fact, it is detective work. Come up to my office, and I'll explain all about it. There's something I want to show you."

2
THE BEAUTIFUL BOOK

Professor McKay got out his ring of keys and unlocked the door to the history building. Then they rode up to the third floor on the elevator, and he unlocked the door to his office. Sitting on his desk was a small, glass case. Professor McKay got out one last key and unlocked the case. Then, with a clean, white cloth, he lifted out a book and let the cousins look at it up close.

"It's beautiful," breathed Sarah-Jane. "But what does it say? I can't read it."

"That's because it's written in Latin," said her uncle. "It's a copy of the Gospel of Matthew. It was made before the printing press was even invented. That means this whole book was copied by hand."

"Wow!" said Timothy. "That must have taken forever!"

"Well, a *long* time, certainly. Books were rare and expensive, so people cherished them. But not all books were as beautiful as this one."

"Look at the little pictures," said Titus. "Is that Jesus?"

"Yes," said his father. "That's Jesus preaching the Sermon on the Mount. You know part of that sermon. You know the Beatitudes."

Titus pointed to a section of graceful printing. "What does that part say?"

His father translated. "It says, 'Blessed are those who hunger and thirst for righteousness, for they will be filled.' It means that people should want more than anything to be good, to be what God wants them to be."

Titus said, "Maybe that's one reason people wanted a copy of the Bible so much—so they could find out what God wanted them to do."

"Good point," agreed his father. "And I think that people today will enjoy seeing this beautiful, old manuscript and thinking of the people long ago, who copied it and loved

13

reading it. But—I must admit I'm a little uneasy about having it on display. It's the most valuable piece in the university's rare book collection. It was Professor Symington's idea to get it out for the fair.

"Then Fred—Professor Symington—discovered that he can't even be here to help with the fair. He made a speaking engagement months ago and forgot all about it until last week. Honestly. He's the original 'absent-minded professor.' So now he's a thousand miles away, and I'm the one worrying about everything."

"How do you want us to help?" asked Titus. "Guard the book?"

"No," said his father, locking the book back in its case. "The security guard will come up with me to get it later. No, I just want you to be on the lookout for any suspicious-looking characters, who might be here to steal the book."

"Uncle Richard," said Timothy. "In these getups, *everybody* is a suspicious-looking character!"

Professor McKay laughed. "Oh, I'm not

worried about the people in costumes—they're all part of the fair. And probably there's nothing to be worried about at all. But just keep your eyes and ears open. And come tell me if there's anything funny going on."

They left the office, and Titus's father locked the door behind them. He locked the door to the history building, too, and they all went back to the fair.

Timothy said, "So let me get this straight. You just want us to walk around, looking like kids."

"Great disguise," said Professor McKay.

"Hey, thanks," said the cousins.

3
WOODEN WHISTLES

Professor McKay had given each cousin some money to spend at the booths, and they each bought exactly the same thing. They each bought a hand-carved, wooden whistle on a long leather thong that could be worn around the neck.

At first they just fooled around with the whistles, trying to see who could get the loudest *TWEEEET*! (Titus.) But then they decided the whistles were too special for that. So they decided to have them be signal-whistles. That way, if one of them wanted to call an emergency meeting of the detective club, he (or she) would blow three times.

After they got it settled about the whistles, there were two other things they wanted to see.

One was a juggler. And the other was a monkey.

Titus said, "My dad told me he hired this really EX-cellent juggler for the fair. He hasn't seen the act himself. But one of my dad's students said this guy is incredible."

No sooner had he said that, than the cousins caught sight of the juggler at the edge of the fairground. His face was painted white like a clown's. He was wearing long, pointy-toed shoes, green tights, a black-and-yellow-checked tunic, and a pointy hood. Over one shoulder he carried a peddler's sack. And his arms were full of juggler's clubs.

Suddenly he tripped over a tree root—or maybe his shoes—and the clubs went flying every which way. The juggler scrambled to pick them up. Then he hurried off behind a nearby tent.

The cousins looked at one another. Finally Timothy said, "So—Uncle Richard hired this guy without actually seeing his act, hmmm?"

Titus groaned. "That's all my dad needs now—an act that bombs. I don't get it. Someone told him the juggler was fantastic. Oh, well. It's too late to do anything about it now."

"Well, maybe dropping his clubs is *part* of the act," suggested Sarah-Jane. But she sounded doubtful about her own suggestion.

"That must be it, . . ." agreed Timothy.

"Let's hope so," said Titus.

4
PIPSQUEAK

The juggler might have been worse than they expected, but the monkey was better than they expected.

He belonged to a friend of Professor McKay's, who owned a pet store.

The man's name was Bill. And the monkey's name was Pipsqueak. (The cousins didn't like to be called pip-squeaks themselves. But for a little monkey, the name sounded sweet and cute. Anyway, Pipsqueak seemed to like it.)

And Pipsqueak really seemed to like it when the cousins petted him. They even got to hold him.

"He just loves attention," Bill explained. "And he's very curious about everything."

"Just like George!" Titus declared. The

Curious George books had been Titus's favorites when he was little. In fact, his parents had even nicknamed Titus "C.G." because Titus was always curious about something.

Titus still went back and reread *Curious George* sometimes. Now he quoted what one of the books said about George: " 'He was a good little monkey, but he was always curious.' "

"That's Pipsqueak," agreed Bill.

"That's sort of us, too," said Sarah-Jane. "The T.C.D.C. is always curious."

"What's a 'teesy-deesy'?" asked Bill.

"It's letters," Timothy explained.

"Capital T.

Capital C.

Capital D.

Capital C.

It stands for the Three Cousins Detective Club."

"Did you hear that, Pipsqueak?" Bill said, "Detectives. You'd better watch yourself now!" Bill explained to the cousins. "Pipsqueak has a bad habit. He's always taking things that don't belong to him."

"Ohhh," said Sarah-Jane as if she were talking to a little baby. "You don't know any better. Do you, Pipsqueak?"

Bill laughed. "Sometimes I wonder. Monkeys are very intelligent, you know. I'm trying to train him not to take things. Actually, I think he thinks he's just bringing me little presents."

"Oh, that's so sweet!" cried Sarah-Jane.

"Hmmm," Bill grunted. "I don't know about that. I'm always having to take things back to people and apologize for my monkey. It's a nuisance." (But the cousins could tell that Bill really loved Pipsqueak anyway.)

Just then another man came hurrying up and said, "Bill, do you know anything about falcons? Apparently all this excitement has been too much for one of the birds. The trainer sure could use a hand."

"I'd be glad to help, but first I have to find someone to watch Pipsqueak."

Titus spoke right up. "We can watch Pipsqueak for you."

Bill looked doubtful.

"Oh, pleeeease!" cried Timothy.

"Oh, pleeeeeeeeeeeeeeease!" cried Sarah-Jane.

"Well, all right..." Bill said slowly.

"EX-cellent!" exclaimed Titus.

"Neat-O!" agreed Timothy.

"So cool!" agreed Sarah-Jane.

"Can we walk around with him?" asked Titus eagerly. "Can we show him the fair?"

Bill said to Pipsqueak, "You'd love that, wouldn't you, boy?" Then he said to the cousins, "But hold onto his leash. Watch him like a hawk. He has 'sticky fingers,' if you know what I mean. I don't want him to get into trouble."

The cousins promised. And Bill said, "OK. Check back with me in about half an hour. Be a good little monkey, Pipsqueak!"

The cousins looked at one another and grinned. They could hardly keep from jumping up and down.

In one morning they had been given three terrific jobs to do:

One—dressing up and being part of the fair.

Two—being on the alert for suspicious-looking visitors.

And three—*monkey-sitting*!

Because there had always been three of them, the cousins had learned to divide by three practically before they could add. But, of course, they couldn't divide a monkey in thirds the way they could a candy bar. So that meant they had to divide the time.

Bill had said to check back in half an hour—thirty minutes. So it wasn't hard to agree that they could each have Pipsqueak for ten minutes.

It wasn't hard to agree that Titus could go first. After all, it was sort of his fair, since his father was in charge of it.

It wasn't even hard to agree that Sarah-Jane could go second. That way it would be boy—girl—boy.

The hard part was doing it.

Pipsqueak was the hardest thing they'd ever had to share.

Pipsqueak wrapped his long arms around Titus's neck, his long legs around Titus's waist, and held on tight. To Titus, the little monkey felt like a cross between a fuzzy toy and a live, cuddly baby. It was as if Curious George himself had stepped right out of the book. Titus wished he could keep Pipsqueak forever.

After they had walked around a little bit, Titus complained, "Honestly, S-J. We're supposed to look like kids looked five hundred years ago."

"So?"

"So people didn't even *have* watches five hundred years ago. So how can we look like the real thing if you keep looking at your watch all the time?"

"You have seven and a half minutes left on your turn," Sarah-Jane replied. "And then it's my turn."

"And after that it's my turn," added Timothy. "In fact, I should probably even get a little bit extra time since I have to go last.''

Titus had to admit to himself that Timothy had a point. But he didn't admit it out loud. Out loud he said, ''And how can we notice suspicious-looking characters if you guys keep looking at S-J's watch all the time?''

''Five minutes,'' said Timothy.

Titus held Pipsqueak a little closer. Pipsqueak was very excited by the fair. He wiggled around and chattered away in monkey-talk that tickled Titus's ear.

And while the cousins were looking at the fair, people were looking at them. Titus heard a preschooler say, ''Mommy! Look! That big boy has a *monkey*!''

Titus couldn't remember when he had ever felt more special.

''Time's up.'' Sarah-Jane's voice broke into his thoughts.

''No,'' said Titus.

''Yes,'' said Sarah-Jane. She held out her wrist.

''She's right, Ti,'' Timothy agreed, checking the watch, just to be sure. ''You have to give S-J

her turn so I can have my turn."

"No!" said Titus.

"What do you mean, 'no'?" asked Sarah-Jane. She sounded annoyed and alarmed all at the same time.

"I mean no, that's all," said Titus. "It's my fair, so I should get to be in charge of the animals."

His cousins stared at him in disbelief. Titus had to admit to himself that it sounded like a pretty stupid excuse. But he didn't admit it out loud.

"That's really rotten, Ti," said Timothy.

"Yeah!" said Sarah-Jane. "We had an *agreement,* Ti!" Her eyes filled with tears of frustration, and she stamped her foot. Sarah-Jane used to do that a lot when she was little. But now, Titus knew, she did it only when she was very, *very* upset.

"Forget you, Ti," muttered Timothy.

"Yeah, Ti," said Sarah-Jane. "Forget you."

They turned and ran away from him.

Titus was never exactly sure what happened next.

Maybe their fight had scared Pipsqueak. Maybe he was impatient to look around some more. Or maybe he just got curious about something.

Whatever it was, Pipsqueak suddenly wriggled out of Titus's arms and scampered off into the crowd.

6
A CALL FOR HELP

For a moment Titus just stood there—frozen in horror.

A kid without a monkey.

Somebody else's monkey.

A monkey that he—Titus—was supposed to be taking care of.

It was a terrible time to be without cousins.

Titus put the little, wooden whistle to his lips and gave three long, desperate blasts.

Sarah-Jane and Timothy came running.

They arrived out of breath and full of questions. "What happened?"

"What's the matter?"

"Where's Pipsqueak?!"

"I lost him," Titus mumbled miserably.

"You WHAT?!"

"I lost Pipsqueak. He just—he just—ran off. And—and I couldn't stop him by myself...."

Sarah-Jane and Timothy were silent, taking in this awful news. Titus wouldn't have blamed them if they'd said, "Good going, Ti," or "We told you so." But they didn't.

"I'm sorry," Titus said. "I'm sorry I wouldn't share. This is all my fault."

"It's just mostly your fault," said Sarah-Jane kindly. "It's not all your fault. I shouldn't have been looking at my watch all the time."

"Yeah," said Timothy. "And we shouldn't have run off and left you alone like that."

Then they all just wanted to forget it and change the subject. They talked about splitting up to cover more ground. But they decided to stay together, because they figured it would take three of them to catch Pipsqueak when they found him.

If they found him.

But they *had* to find him. They just had to. It was the most frantic-feeling hunt they had ever been on.

But, in the end, it was Pipsqueak who found them.

They were looking in the opposite direction when Pipsqueak scampered up with a present for Sarah-Jane. Perhaps he thought he was a knight in shining armor bringing a little gift to his fair lady. But he spoiled the effect when he dropped it on her foot.

"OW!" cried Sarah-Jane, hopping up and down on her good foot. "Ow, ow, ow, ow, ow!" But then, when she realized what had happened, she gasped, "Oh, Pipsqueak! Am I ever glad to see *you*!"

Timothy snatched up Pipsqueak's leash before the little monkey could get any more crazy ideas about running off.

Titus stooped down to pick up Pipsqueak's present.

It was a juggler's club.

The cousins stared at one another in dismay. Sticky-Fingers Pipsqueak had been at it again.

7
THE JUGGLER'S CLUB

"Oh, no," Sarah-Jane groaned. "You're in trouble now, Pipsqueak."

"It's a disaster," Titus muttered.

"Maybe not," said Timothy. "Maybe if we get the club back to the juggler right away, he'll be OK about it. We can explain that Pipsqueak doesn't understand he's not supposed to take things."

Sarah-Jane and Titus brightened up at this suggestion. Now that the enormous disaster of losing Pipsqueak was over, it was almost fun to have an ordinary disaster to straighten out. It was Sarah-Jane's turn to hold Pipsqueak, but she and Timothy switched turns. That way, she could hide the club in the folds of her long skirt. (They didn't want everyone knowing what Pipqueak had been up to.)

They set off in search of the juggler. He wasn't hard to find. They found him performing for a delighted group of visitors. The juggler's face was painted white like a clown's. He was wearing long, pointy-toed shoes, red tights, a black-and-white-checked tunic, and a pointy hood. He managed to keep six brightly colored balls spinning up and down through the air. And he never dropped a single one.

The cousins stood back a little way from the audience and waited for a chance to talk to the juggler in private.

"He's good," Titus whispered to his cousins. "I mean, he's *really good*."

"Yeah," said Timothy thoughtfully. "I wonder why he looked so clumsy before?"

"What *I* wonder," said Sarah-Jane, "is why he changed his costume."

The boys stared at her.

Sarah-Jane sighed impatiently. "Just *once*, gentlemen, I wish you would pay attention to what people are wearing." She tossed her head as she said this to show off the ribbons.

Now it was the boys' turn to sigh impatiently. "What are you getting at, S-J?"

Sarah-Jane shrugged. "I don't know. All I know is that when we saw the juggler before, his tights were green, and his tunic was black and yellow."

The boys looked back at the juggler and blinked in surprise. Now his tights were red, and his tunic was black and white.

It was certainly odd. But there was no time to think about it. The juggler was smiling and bowing. The audience was laughing and clapping.

The audience drifted away to see other shows, and the juggler took a break.

The cousins hurried over to him. Sarah-Jane drew the club from the folds of her skirt and held it out to the juggler.

All in a rush she said, "Sir, we just want to return this to you. Our monkey took it. But he doesn't really know any better yet. So—could you please not tell on him? We're trying to keep him out of trouble."

The juggler made a sweeping bow to Sarah-Jane. "I am your humble servant, milady. I will guard your secret with my life. But that is not my club."

"But—but we saw you!" cried Timothy. "You were carrying an arm load of clubs, and you dropped them all over the place."

The juggler clapped his hand over his heart and staggered back, horrified. "Young man, I do not drop things."

A new thought suddenly occurred to Titus. "Then my dad must have hired another juggler."

"Nope," said the juggler. "Professor McKay told me I would be paid extra because I would be so busy. And the reason I would be so busy is that I would be the only juggler."

It was time for the juggler to start another show, and there didn't seem to be any more he could tell them. So the cousins wandered away.

The morning was not staying as good as it had started off. They still hadn't given the club back. Sarah-Jane had hardly had any time with Pipsqueak. And it was almost time to check back with Bill.

Titus had an idea. "Let's put the club back where we first saw the juggler. Maybe when he sees that he's missing a club, he'll go back to the place where he dropped them. Then let's ask Bill if we can have some more time with Pipsqueak, so that Sarah-Jane can still have her whole turn. Then we can go on looking for the other juggler. And there *is* another juggler. We didn't just imagine him."

"Right," said Sarah-Jane. "Because where else did Pipsqueak get the club?"

"Right," said Timothy. "And while we're looking for the juggler, we can still do our other job. We can still be on the lookout for suspicious-looking strangers."

"Right," said Titus and Sarah-Jane.

When they checked back with Bill, they saw that he had helped to get the nervous falcon calmed down. But now—he was trying to get

Titus's father to calm down.

The cousins rushed over.

"What's the matter, Uncle Richard?"

"What's wrong?"

"Dad! What happened?"

Professor McKay wrung his hands and paced up and down. "It's gone. The Gospel is gone."

The cousins could hardly believe their ears.

"But how?" they asked. "Who?"

Professor McKay shook his head. "I wish I knew! The security guard and I just went up to my office to get the book. The case was open. And the book was gone."

"But I don't understand, Dad. The building was locked. Your office was locked. The case was locked."

The security guard said, "It must have been an inside job by someone who was able to get hold of the keys."

"But *who*?" cried Professor McKay.

Titus glanced at his cousins. "Dad? We don't know who took it, but—"

"No, of course you don't, Son. That's all right."

"No, Dad. What I mean is, we don't know who took it, because he was wearing a really good disguise."

"The *juggler*!" cried Timothy and Sarah-Jane together as they saw what Titus was getting at.

"The *juggler*?" asked Professor McKay, completely puzzled. "What are you guys talking about? The juggler is a fine young man, who—"

"No, Dad. Not *that* juggler. The *other* juggler."

"*What* other juggler? Son, you're not making any sense. There's only one."

"There's only one *real* juggler," replied Titus. "The clumsy juggler is a fake."

"Whoever heard of a clumsy juggler?" asked Bill.

"Our point exactly," said Titus. He told them about seeing the juggler drop his clubs.

40

Sarah-Jane described exactly what the fake juggler was wearing.

And Timothy said, "What are we waiting for? He's going to get away!"

Professor McKay quickly called together a group of helpers. Then they all split up to search the fair for a mysterious, clumsy juggler.

Timothy, Titus, and Sarah-Jane stayed together, and Pipsqueak went with them. (He had been glad to see Bill again, of course, but he was like a kid playing at his friend's house. He didn't want to "go home" yet.)

So the cousins took him with them on the search.

And it was the cousins and Pipsqueak who saw the juggler first.

Professor McKay had warned them not to try to stop the juggler themselves.

So they put their whistles in their mouths, and they blew and blew and blew.

The juggler realized that the whistles were a signal. He tried to run away, but he got tangled up in his pointy-toed shoes and fell down. Almost instantly he was surrounded by

Professor McKay's helpers and curious visitors, who thought it was all part of the show.

Before Sarah-Jane could stop him, Pipsqueak scampered up to the juggler and grabbed the peddler's sack. The juggler lunged for it, but Pipsqueak was too fast for him. The little knight brought the sack straight to his fair lady. And dropped it on her foot.

"OW!" cried Sarah-Jane, hopping up and down on her good foot. "Ow, ow, ow, ow, ow! What's in there, Pipsqueak?"

"I think we know," said Titus. He opened

the sack just as his father rushed up. "I was right, Dad. Here's the Gospel. And there's the thief. It was the fake juggler, all right. But we still don't know who he is."

Professor McKay looked closely at the clumsy juggler and said with deep sadness, "I do. It's my friend—Professor Fred Symington."

"I still can't believe it," Professor McKay said later. He and Bill and the cousins and Pipsqueak were having lunch in the refreshments tent. "I knew Fred Symington was crazy about that book. I guess you could say he had a *hunger* for it. Of course, he could get a pass from me to study the book whenever he wanted. But apparently that wasn't enough for him. He wanted to own it. But he couldn't just take the book, because the department keeps close track of who is using it. And he couldn't get hold of a key to the library to sneak in and get it. So he had to figure out another way to get his hands on it."

Timothy said, "So he got the idea of having the Gospel on display at the fair. He figured he could get his hands on it then."

"That's right," said his uncle. "He knew I was going to keep the book in my office until it was time to bring it down to the fair. Fred already had a key to the history building. Somehow, he got hold of my keys and made a copy of the key to my office. He just picked the lock on the case."

Professor McKay continued, "Fred knew no one would ever suspect him, because he was supposed to be a thousand miles away at the time of the fair. But, of course, there never was any speaking engagement. He just made that up."

Sarah-Jane said, "But he couldn't just come here, as himself. Someone would see him and recognize him. So he had to have a disguise." She nodded. "And that was sort of smart. Because if you dressed up like an old-time juggler and walked down a regular street, you would really be a suspicious-looking character. But if you dressed up like an old-time juggler and walked around an old-time fair, you wouldn't be suspicious-looking at all!"

"He was pretty smart, all right," said her

uncle. But it didn't sound like Professor McKay thought it was a good kind of smartness.

Titus said quietly, "Professor Symington may have hungered after that old copy of the Gospel of Matthew. But he didn't do what the book said. He didn't 'hunger and thirst after righteousness.' "

His father nodded. "You're right about that, Titus. It seems to me that Fred Symington completely missed the point. He appreciated one kind of value in that beautiful, old book. But he didn't understand the deeper value—doing what the book says."

They were all silent for a moment. All except Pipsqueak, that is. He didn't really understand what was going on. All he knew was that he wasn't getting enough attention. He bounced from cousin to cousin, chattering and doing tricks.

Bill laughed and said, "I think that Pipsqueak wants to be in the detective club."

"Oh, I don't know if he can," said Professor McKay. He winked at the cousins. "Because—when it comes to solving mysteries—the

T.C.D.C. doesn't monkey around."

The End

THE TEN COMMANDMENTS MYSTERIES

When Timothy, Titus, and Sarah-Jane, the three cousins, get together the most ordinary events turn into mysteries. So they've formed the T.C.D.C. (That's the Three Cousins Detective Club.)

And while the three cousins are solving mysteries, they're also learning about the Ten Commandments and living God's way.

You'll want to solve all ten mysteries along with Sarah-Jane, Ti, and Tim:

The Mystery of the Laughing Cat—"You shall not steal." *Someone stole rare coins. Can the cousins find the thief?*

The Mystery of the Messed-up Wedding—"You shall not commit adultery." *Can the cousins find the missing wedding ring?*

The Mystery of the Gravestone Riddle—"You shall not murder." *Can the cousins solve a 100-year-old murder case?*

The Mystery of the Carousel Horse—"You shall not covet." *Why does the stranger want an old, wooden horse?*

The Mystery of the Vanishing Present—"Remember the Sabbath day and keep it holy." *Can the cousins figure out who has Grandpa's missing birthday gift?*

The Mystery of the Silver Dolphin—"You shall not give false testimony." *Who's telling the truth—and who's lying?*

The Mystery of the Tattletale Parrot—"You shall not misuse the name of the Lord your God." *What will the beautiful green parrot say next?*

The Mystery of the Second Map—"You shall have no other gods before me." *Can the cousins discover who dropped the strange map?*

The Mystery of the Double Trouble—"Honor your father and your mother." *How could Timothy be in two places at once?*

The Mystery of the Silent Idol—"You shall not make for yourself an idol." *If the idol could speak, what would it tell the cousins?*

Available at your local Christian bookstore.

David C. Cook Publishing Co., Elgin, IL 60120